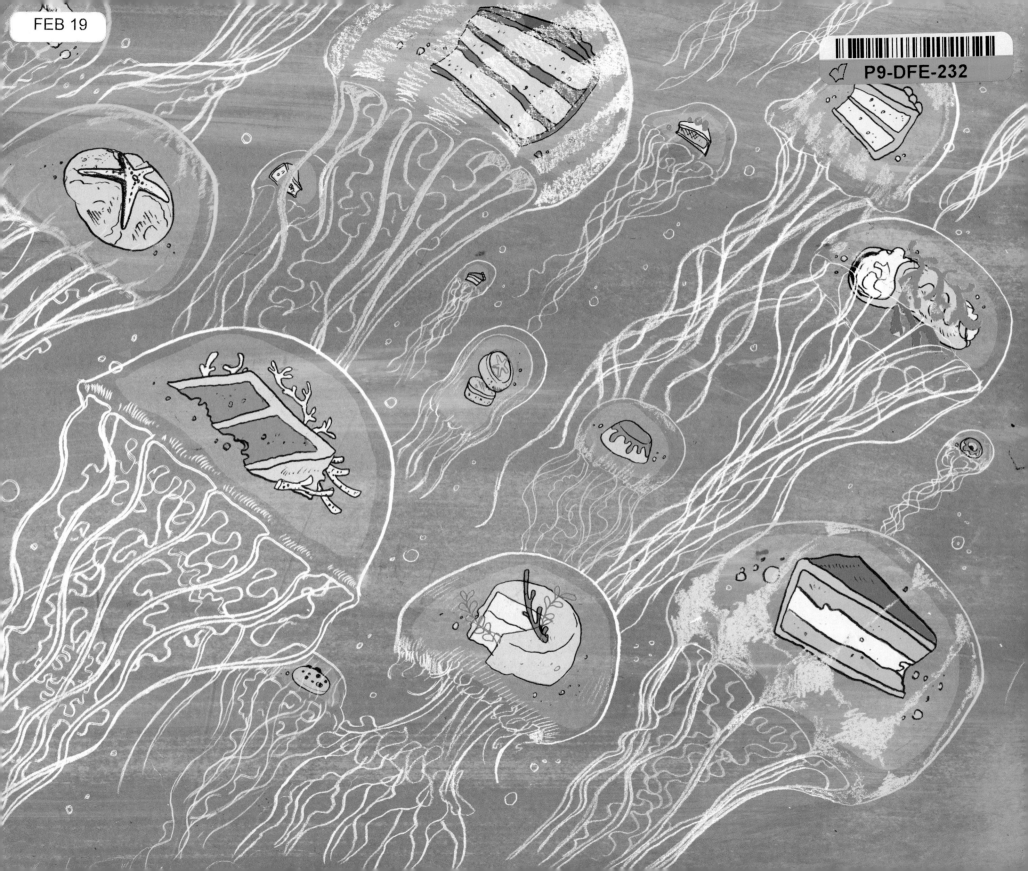

For my family

hmhco.com

The illustrations in this book were done using graphite on Bristol vellum and digital color.
The text type was set in Andrea Tsurumi's handwriting.
The display type was hand-lettered by Andrea Tsurumi.

Library of Congress Cataloging-in-Publication Data is on file.

ISBN: 978-0-544-95900-2

Manufactured in China
SCP 10 9 8 7 6 5 4 3 2 1
4500738664

CRAB CAKE

TURNING THE TIDE TOGETHER

ANDREA TSURUMI

Houghton Mifflin Harcourt
Boston   New York

Under the sea, where sunlight touches sand, lies a place that's home to many incredible creatures.

Manta Ray gets cleaned.

Clownfish hides in the stinging anemone (ah-neh-mo-nee).

Tangs swim in schools.

Scallop does
loop-de-loops.

Sea Turtle
holds her
breath.

And Crab bakes cakes.

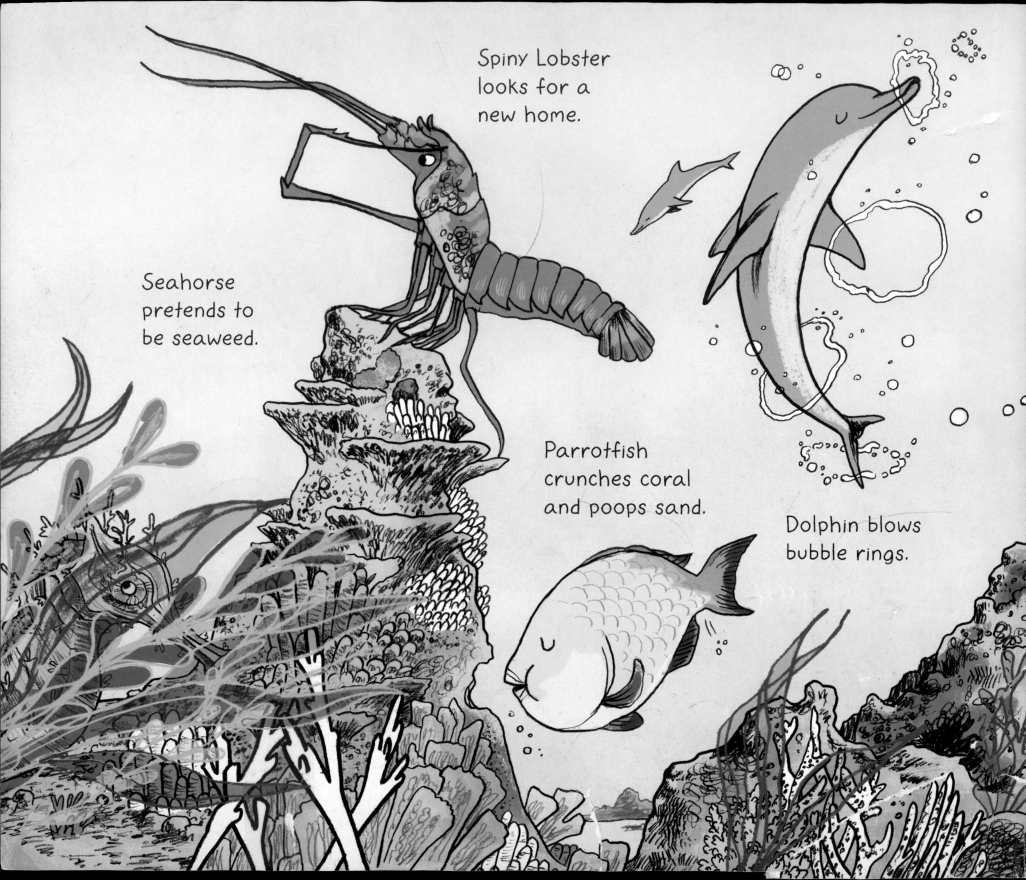

Spiny Lobster looks for a new home.

Seahorse pretends to be seaweed.

Parrotfish crunches coral and poops sand.

Dolphin blows bubble rings.

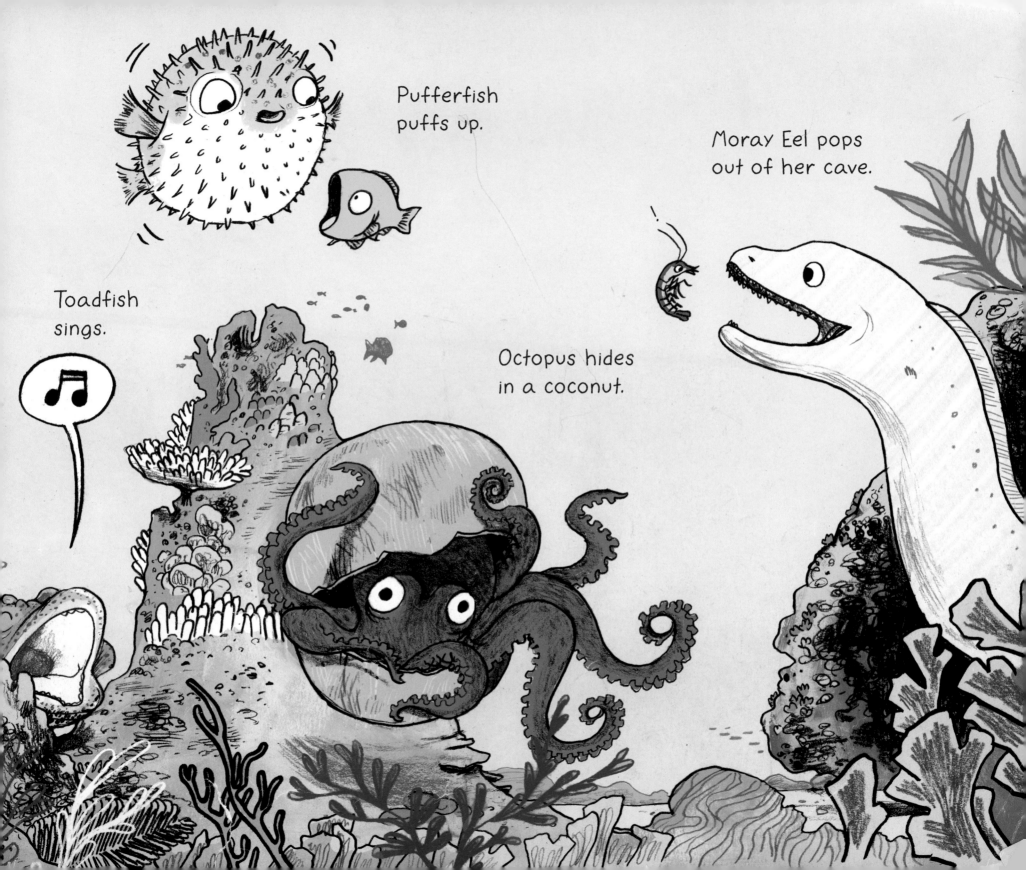

Pufferfish
puffs up.

Moray Eel pops
out of her cave.

Toadfish
sings.

Octopus hides
in a coconut.

And Crab bakes cakes.

The venomous Lionfish does whatever she pleases.

And Crab bakes cakes.

So life goes on
under the sea.

Until one night,
there's a
BIG SPLASH!

Parrotfish
freezes.

Clownfish
freezes.

Snapper
freezes.

Spiny Lobster
freezes.

Shark
freezes.

Pufferfish
freezes.

Seahorse
freezes.

Sea Turtle freezes.

Dolphin freezes.

Manta Ray freezes.

Octopus freezes.

Even Lionfish freezes.

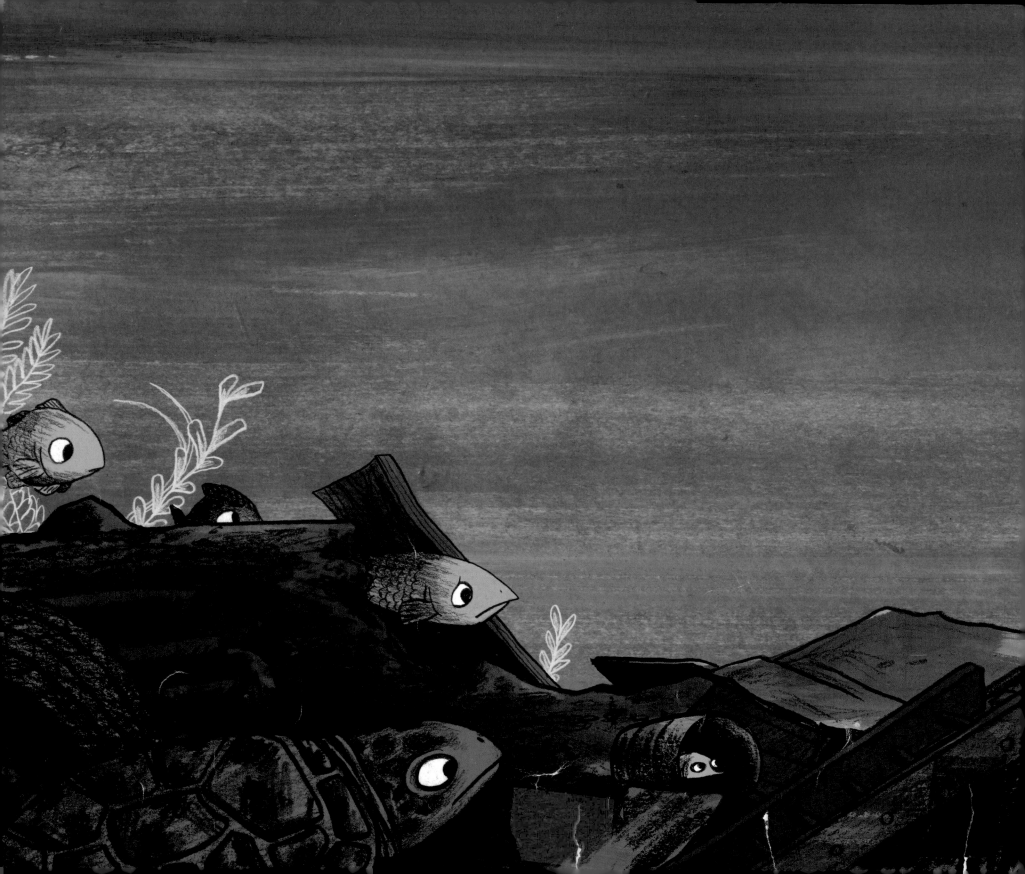

Crab bakes a cake.

Lobster  lifts. 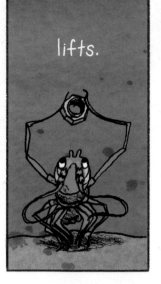 Snapper shoves.  Clownfish rolls.

Manta Rays move.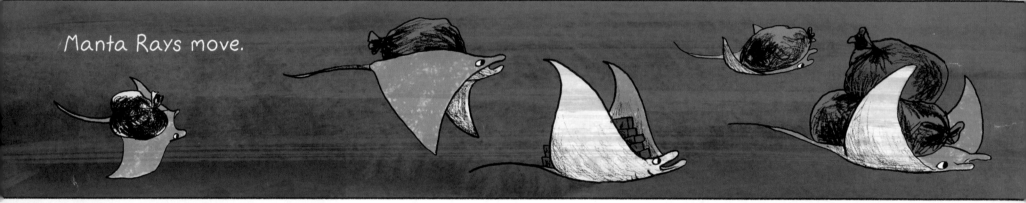

Octopus inks.  Sharks carry

Turtles tow.

Dolphins drag.

Clam encourages.

and Sea Lions lug.

Under the sea, where sunlight still touches sand,
incredible creatures go on swimming,
playing, and doing what they do.

Especially Crab.

NASA Climate Kids Ocean Resources:
climatekids.nasa.gov/menu/ocean

Thank You Ocean Kid Zone:
thankyouocean.org/kid-zone

National Institute of Environmental
Health Sciences Pollution Page:
kids.niehs.nih.gov/topics/pollution/index.htm

National Geographic's
#PlanetorPlastic initiative:
nationalgeographic.com/
environment/planetorplastic/

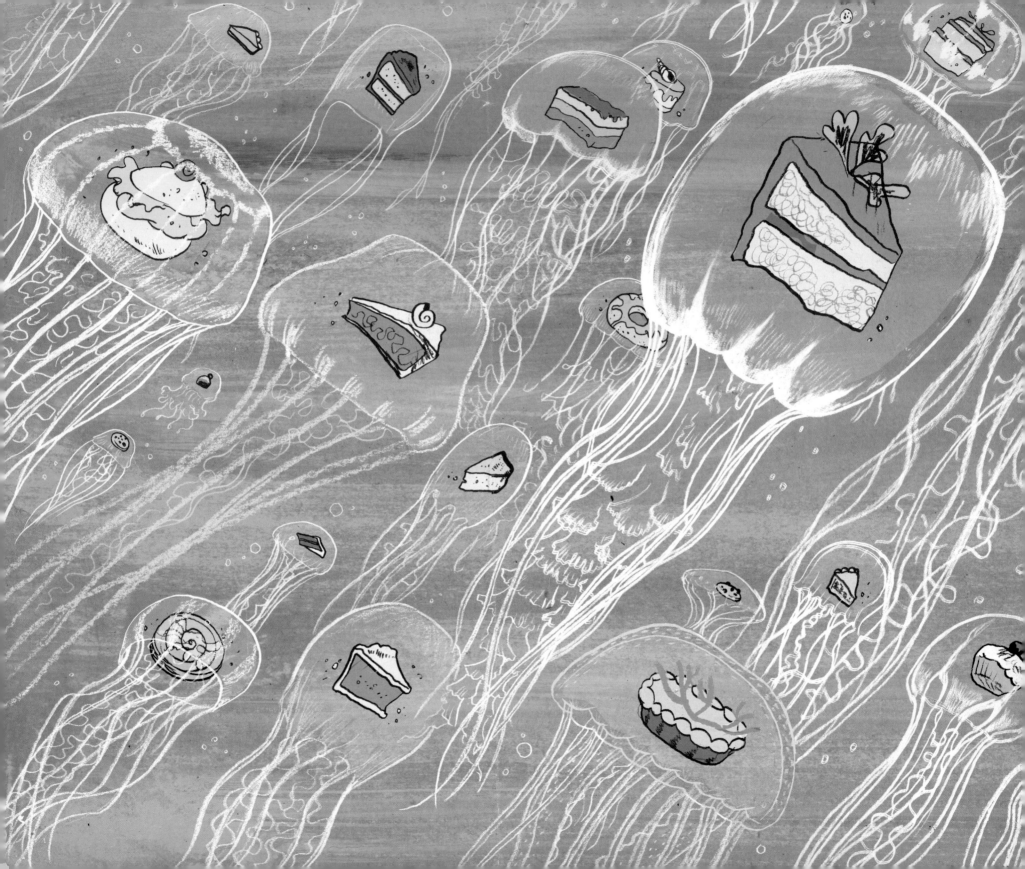